King of Diamonds?

Bert edged closer to Mr. Bascomb's brief-case. He could plainly see the bag of glittering gems inside.

It was now or never, and Bert had to think fast. Before Mr. Bascomb could react, Bert pretended to lose his balance. Then he "acci-dentally" kicked the briefcase over. Just as he had hoped, the sparkling little stones went fly-ing. They spilled all over the floor.

"The diamonds!" Freddie and Flossie s… …nd

…ht

Books in The New Bobbsey Twins series

1 The Secret of Jungle Park
2 The Case of the Runaway Money
3 The Clue That Flew Away
4 The Secret in the Sand Castle
5 The Case of the Close Encounter
6 Mystery on the Mississippi
7 Trouble in Toyland
8 The Secret of the Stolen Puppies
9 The Clue in the Classroom
#10 The Chocolate-Covered Clue
#11 The Case of the Crooked Contest
#12 The Secret of the Sunken Treasure
#13 The Case of the Crying Clown
#14 The Mystery of the Missing Mummy
#15 The Secret of the Stolen Clue

Available from MINSTREL Books

LAURA LEE HOPE

ILLUSTRATED BY PAUL JENNIS

PUBLISHED BY POCKET BOOKS

New York London Toronto Sydney Tokyo

A MINSTREL PAPERBACK *ORIGINAL*

A Minstrel Book, published by
POCKET BOOKS, a division of Simon & Schuster Inc.
1230 Avenue of the Americas, New York, NY 10020

Produced by Mega-Books of New York, Inc.

ISBN: 0-671-67596-6

First Minstrel Books Printing December 1989

10 9 8 7 6 5 4 3 2 1

Printed in the U.S.A.

Contents

THE SECRET OF THE STOLEN CLUE

1

The Birthday Smash

"Mom is going to love this birthday present," twelve-year-old Nan Bobbsey said happily. She carefully set the glass dog down in the cardboard box on her bed.

"It looks just like Chief," her younger sister, Flossie, said proudly.

Chief was the Bobbsey twins' lovable sheepdog puppy. He cocked his head and stared at the present with a funny look on his face. Flossie laughed because it was the same look that was on the face of the glass pooch.

"We'd better hurry and get it wrapped," said

Nan's twin brother, Bert. "Mom is in a big rush this morning to get to work."

"It's terrible that she has to work on her birthday," complained Flossie.

"Yeah," agreed Bert. "And even worse, it's Saturday! It's a good thing she likes her job."

"Let's just hope she also likes her birthday present," said Nan. She closed the box around the delicate glass dog.

"I'll get the ribbon," offered Flossie.

"And I'll get the tape," said Bert.

Flossie raced back across the room with a handful of bright red ribbon. Chief wagged his tail.

Just then, the door crashed open and Flossie's twin brother, Freddie, barreled into the room—and right into Flossie. The ribbon went flying. It landed in a swirl of loops all around Chief's head.

The twins' dog cheerfully began to tear at the ribbon with his teeth.

Meanwhile, Nan and Bert picked the younger twins up off the rug. "Are you guys okay?" asked Nan.

"I'm just fine. Except I have a jerk for a brother," said Flossie, glaring at Freddie.

"Hey, it was an accident," Freddie said. "Be-

sides, you wanted me to tell you when Mom was leaving. And she left!"

Bert looked at his new Rex Sleuther Detecto watch and shook his head in disbelief. "We blew it. Mom left twenty minutes early. Dad's picking her up at the newspaper after work to celebrate her birthday. They won't be home until late."

"What are we going to do?" asked Freddie. "We spent all of our savings on that glass dog. Now we can't even give it to Mom on her birthday."

"Yes, we can!" said Nan with a determination that the others knew well.

"How?" asked Flossie.

"We'll wrap up the present, then bike over to the newspaper and give it to her there," Nan announced. "Mom would never expect us to show up at her office, and—"

"It'll be a terrific surprise," Bert broke in, leaping into the air with new enthusiasm. "Let's do it!"

"All right!" shouted Freddie.

"Yeah!" cried Flossie.

"Woof!" Chief barked loudly and ran around in a circle.

* * *

Nan snatched the brightly gift-wrapped box from the basket on her bicycle. Bert was already holding open the front door to the *Lakeport News* building.

"Hurry up!" he called. "Flossie and Freddie are getting way ahead of us."

When Nan reached Bert, she gave him the package. "The whole way over here I was scared that this would break," she said. "You carry it the rest of the way, okay?"

"Sure," said Bert.

Then Nan and Bert took off after the younger twins as they raced for their mother's office.

"Mom!" Flossie cried with glee. She skidded to a stop outside Mrs. Bobbsey's open office door. "Guess what?"

"Flossie, what in the world are you doing here?" Mrs. Bobbsey asked, getting up from behind her desk.

"Hi, Mom!" Freddie said, sticking his head inside the office.

"You, too?" Mrs. Bobbsey said, shaking her head. "You know, something tells me you two aren't alone."

"Good guess," said Flossie.

With that, Bert and Nan appeared in the

doorway. All four twins crowded into their mother's office.

"You'll have to excuse my children," Mrs. Bobbsey said to a surprised young man. He was sitting in a chair with a notebook on his lap.

"Oh, we didn't know you were busy," Nan said sheepishly. "Do you want us to wait outside?"

"No, that's okay," Mrs. Bobbsey answered with a smile. "Amos Fenster, here, is our new crime reporter. I was just telling him that he might not have much to write about in Lakeport. It's a quiet town."

Amos Fenster, a tall, skinny young man with a mop of unruly red hair, laughed harshly. "If a town is quiet, it just means that the villains are sneaky. But if they're here, I'll find them," he said. He swept his arm out in a wide arc and knocked a tall stack of papers off Mrs. Bobbsey's desk.

"Oh, sorry," he said, scrambling to the floor. He began to pick up the papers, scanning them quickly as he shuffled them back into a pile.

The Bobbseys started to help, but he shooed them away. "I've got them," he said. "No harm done."

As Mr. Fenster was kneeling on the floor, he

turned his back to the twins for a moment. Then he stood up and put the papers back on Mrs. Bobbsey's desk, smiling a little bit. "Looks like everybody's waiting for that last clue in tomorrow's paper," he said. "For that big diamond contest, I mean. I heard that twice as many newspapers have been sold every Sunday since the contest started."

"Mom says that diamonds are a newspaper's best friend," Flossie piped up.

"It's amazing that nobody has found those diamonds yet," Amos Fenster said thoughtfully. He sat down, staring at the pile of papers he had just put back on Mrs. Bobbsey's desk.

"The clues have been really hard," said Nan.

"Yeah," agreed Bert. "There have been eleven of them, and so far they've stumped everybody."

"I didn't understand the last one at all," Freddie admitted. "It was, 'Go to the place where people are both shallow and deep.' What does that mean?"

"If we knew," said Bert, "we'd find those diamonds in a second."

Amos Fenster laughed. "Well, it's going to be a wild scramble when that last clue comes out. Five thousand dollars in diamonds! The final clue ought to make sense of all the other clues."

Mrs. Bobbsey frowned suddenly. "I can't believe it," she said, shaking her head. "Mr. Cooper, the publisher, came by with his daughter when I arrived this morning. He gave me the clue in a sealed envelope. But I've been so busy writing my story for tomorrow's paper that I haven't sent it over yet to the managing editor. She's the one who'll make sure it gets printed."

Amos Fenster stood up. "Oh, you've got plenty of time," he said. "We don't go to press until five o'clock, right?"

"On the job two days and you know all the deadlines," Mrs. Bobbsey said with a smile.

Mr. Fenster grinned. Then he waved at the children and walked out the door.

"You're not angry that we came to your office, are you, Mom?" Bert asked after Amos Fenster was gone.

"I won't be angry," Mrs. Bobbsey teased, "if that box is my birthday present."

The twins laughed. "Surprise!" they said all together.

Flossie wanted to be the one to give their mother the present. She grabbed the box with its polka-dot paper and red ribbons out of Bert's hands.

Freddie reached for the box a moment later.

He also wanted to hand the present to their mother. Freddie managed to get his hands on the box and pull it away from Flossie. But only for a second.

"Let go!" Flossie demanded, tugging at the package.

"You let go," Freddie told her, pulling at his end of the box.

"No. I'm giving it to Mom," Flossie insisted.

"Who says?"

"Look out!" Nan shouted. But it was too late. Flossie and Freddie both lost their grip on the box, and it crashed to the floor. Everyone heard the sound of breaking glass.

"Uh-oh," said Flossie, covering her face with her hands.

Freddie looked down at the floor, feeling about as tall as his shoelaces.

"Nice going, guys," said Bert.

Flossie bent down to open the box, but Nan stopped her. "It's probably full of broken glass," she said. "You might get hurt."

"It's the thought that counts," Mrs. Bobbsey said quickly. "It was very nice of you to buy me a present."

"Chief helped," said Flossie sadly. "He licked the envelope."

Bert lifted an envelope from the floor, where

it lay with the shattered present. He gave it to his mother.

Mrs. Bobbsey opened the envelope and took out the birthday card. She smiled after she read it. "Thanks," she said. "This is really sweet. I'll put it on my desk so everyone can see it. And don't worry about the present. Now, you had all better get going so I can get back to work."

The twins kissed their mother goodbye and shuffled out of her office.

"Some birthday present," mumbled Nan.

"Yeah, a pile of broken glass," agreed Bert in a whisper. He closed the door behind them. "I wish there were something we could do to make up for it."

"Next year we'll do something extra special for Mom," said Nan, trying to cheer her brother up.

Farther down the hall, Flossie and Freddie walked side by side. They didn't look at each other. Finally, though, Flossie said in a small voice, "I feel terrible."

"Me, too," whispered Freddie.

They were halfway down the hall when a loud cry stopped them dead in their tracks. It had come from their mother's office!

2

Without a Clue

With Bert and Nan in the lead, the twins rushed back to their mother's office.

"It's gone!" Mrs. Bobbsey cried as she grabbed at the papers on her desk.

"What happened, Mom?" Nan asked. "What's gone?"

Bert, Flossie, and Freddie stood behind their sister in the doorway. They watched as their mother pounded her fist on the desktop. They had rarely seen her so upset.

"Someone stole the last clue for the diamond contest," Mrs. Bobbsey said finally. She slumped into her chair. "Mr. Cooper, the publisher, gave it to me less than an hour ago. I put it down right here." She pointed to the front corner of the desk near where Mr. Fenster had sat. "If that clue doesn't appear in tomorrow's paper, the contest will be ruined. And I'll probably be out of a job."

"Can't you just call the publisher and get a new copy of the clue?" asked Bert.

Mrs. Bobbsey looked at her watch and shook her head. "Mr. Cooper's plane takes off for Hawaii in ten minutes. There's no way to reach him before five o'clock. That's when tomorrow's edition of the *Lakeport News* goes to press," she added sadly.

Nan hated seeing her mom so unhappy. "Don't worry," she said. "We'll find the creep who stole that clue."

"That's right," added Flossie. "And we'll get that clue back before the paper gets pressed."

"Not 'pressed,'" Bert corrected her.

"Ironed?" asked Flossie.

"A newspaper *goes to press* when all the news is printed on paper," explained Bert patiently.

"Well," said Flossie quickly, "we'll get the clue back by then."

"It'll be our birthday present to you," Freddie told his mother. "Right, guys?"

"Right!" they all shouted together.

Mrs. Bobbsey's eyes filled with tears. "You kids have solved a lot of cases," she said. "But don't get your hopes up too high about solving this one. I have no idea who could have taken the envelope with the clue. And there's so little time. I don't see how you can get to the bottom of this before five o'clock."

"We've got to try," said Nan.

"I can't even help you," said Mrs. Bobbsey with a sigh. "I have to write a special article about the mayor for tomorrow's paper."

"You write the story, and we'll find the clue," said Bert. He checked his Rex Sleuther Detecto watch. It was twenty minutes to twelve. That left just five hours and twenty minutes to find both the thief and the clue. There was no time to waste.

"We need to know exactly what happened after Mr. Cooper gave you the clue," said Nan.

Mrs. Bobbsey thought for a moment. "After Mr. Cooper and his daughter, Suzy, came in, I put the envelope with the clue on my desk under my favorite paperweight," she said. She pointed to the wooden heart that Bert had carved years before in summer camp. "Then I walked with Mr. Cooper to the door and wished him a good trip."

"Did you go back to your desk?" asked Bert.

"No. I had to pick something up at the art department." Mrs. Bobbsey frowned. "I came back about ten minutes later. When I turned the corner in the hallway, I thought I saw Helen Crane, the fashion editor, coming out of my office. She was probably dropping off her column for me to read."

"Then what did you do?" asked Nan.

Mrs. Bobbsey shrugged. "I came in here and worked on my article until Amos stopped in. And I really have to finish it before we go to press today. It's just as important as finding that clue." She put a hand to her forehead. "What a birthday!" she said.

There was a knock at the door. A tall, chubby man stuck his head into the office. "Excuse me, Mrs. Bobbsey," he said. "The photos of the mayor are ready. Do you want to take a look?"

"I'm sorry, kids, but I've got to go to the photo department," said Mrs. Bobbsey. "I do wish that I could help you find that stolen clue. Try your best, but don't be too disappointed if it's gone for good. And, please, don't get in anybody's way. Okay?"

"Don't worry," said Nan. "We'll solve the case *and* stay out of trouble."

Bert looked at Flossie and Freddie. "Well,

most of us will stay out of trouble," he said with a grin.

As soon as Mrs. Bobbsey had left with the man, the twins went into a huddle.

"What are we going to do now?" asked Flossie. "We'll never find that clue by five o'clock."

"We promised Mom we'd try," said Nan.

Bert nodded. "One thing is for sure," he said. "This is an inside job. The thief has to be someone on the newspaper staff."

"How do you know that?" Freddie asked.

Bert shrugged. "That's simple. Only people who work at the paper could know that Mr. Cooper had given the clue to Mom."

"But which ones?" asked Freddie.

"That's what we've got to find out," said Nan. "And there is one suspicious person I can think of: Helen Crane, the fashion editor. I bet she took the clue with her when she dropped off her column."

"What about that crime reporter?" suggested Bert. "He was in here, too. Maybe he stole the envelope with the clue when he knocked over all those papers on Mom's desk."

"Yeah," Flossie agreed. "It was probably him, all right. Nobody could be that clumsy. Not even Freddie."

"Thanks a lot," said her twin, throwing her a dirty look.

"To save time," Nan said, "let's split up into pairs. That way, we can go after both of our suspects at the same time."

"I'll go with Bert," offered Flossie.

"I guess that means you're stuck with me," Nan kidded Freddie.

"Nope," said Freddie. "It's the thief who stole that clue from Mom who's stuck with *us.*"

"That's the spirit!" said Nan. "Let's go!"

Bert asked a mail clerk in the corridor outside their mother's office how they could find Amos Fenster.

"Just enter that maze of little cubicles," he said. "That's where most of the reporters work. Make three rights and then a left. You can't miss Mr. Fenster. He has his name up on the wall."

With Flossie tagging along behind him, Bert followed the clerk's directions. At almost every desk they passed, people were working at their computer screens.

When he and Flossie made the final turn, Bert saw the name *Amos Fenster* on the outside of a partition separating the reporters' little offices.

"Let me do the talking," Bert whispered to Flossie. "You keep an eye out for anything suspicious. Okay?"

She nodded.

As they neared the opening to Mr. Fenster's cubicle, Bert tried to think of a question that would catch the crime reporter off guard. Instead, Bert was the one surprised when he heard a voice from inside the cubicle say, "They'll never figure it was me. Never!"

3

Trouble Ahead

"We've practically caught Mr. Fenster red-handed!" declared Bert. "Come on!"

He and Flossie raced to the open doorway of the crime reporter's cubicle. Then they marched right in on the unsuspecting Amos Fenster.

"Thought you could get away with it, huh?" Flossie put her hands on her hips.

Hearing the voice behind him, the reporter quickly hung up the phone. He dropped what he had in his hands. Then he spun around in his chair to face Bert and Flossie.

"What are you kids doing here?" Mr. Fenster asked angrily.

"Catching you admitting your crime," Bert announced.

"What crime? What are you talking about?" the reporter asked. "I've heard that you Bobbseys solve mysteries, but I find that hard to believe. Do you just go around accusing people of things?"

"Don't play dumb," said Bert. "My sister and I both heard you admit it before we came in here."

"Admit what?" Mr. Fenster asked.

"That you stole the diamond contest clue from our mom's office," said Flossie. "Give it back," she demanded, holding out her hand.

Amos Fenster threw back his head and laughed. His Adam's apple bounced up and down in his throat.

"What's so funny?" Bert asked, confused.

"Your mother just told me that there's hardly any crime in Lakeport. And now, all of a sudden, we've got ourselves a major theft."

"Yeah, and we heard you confess to it," said Bert.

"Me? Don't be silly," Mr. Fenster scoffed.

"What you heard was me reading to my nephew over the phone. He's sick at home. He wanted to know what happened in the latest Rex Sleuther comic book."

"Your nephew's a Rex Sleuther fan?" Bert asked, surprised.

"Not only is he a fan, but I am, too," the crime reporter replied. He picked up a comic book from his desk. Then he opened it to the page he had been reading. "Take a look," Mr. Fenster said smugly. He handed the book to Bert and pointed to a balloon over the comic book villain's head.

Bert grimaced as he read aloud, " 'They'll never figure it was me. Never!' " He closed the comic book and shrugged. "Okay," he said. "You didn't confess to stealing the diamond clue. But that still doesn't prove that you didn't take it."

"Right," said Flossie. "For someone who says he's innocent, you sure acted real guilty when we came in here."

"Well, you're right about that," Mr. Fenster confessed. "The fact is, I thought I'd been caught reading from a comic book by my boss. That would have been really embarrassing. I'm glad it was only you Bobbseys." Then he

brightened. "And I'm especially glad you told me about the stolen diamond clue. You're sure it's really been stolen?"

"Oh, yes," Flossie said.

"Great!" Mr. Fenster said gleefully. "It'll make a terrific story!" He banged his fist on the arm of his chair. "I'm going to crack this case. And I'm sorry to say this, kids, but the main suspect has got to be your mother."

Bert was stunned. Flossie's eyes went wide, and her mouth fell open. At first, neither twin could speak.

"Sure," continued the reporter. "She probably took the clue herself, is claiming it was stolen, and plans to sneak off with the diamonds."

"Hey!" demanded Flossie, stamping her foot on the floor. "How can you say that about my mom?"

"Because he's nuts!" Bert blurted out. "To think that our mother could have stolen that clue is ridiculous!"

"Rex Sleuther doesn't rule out *any* suspects," Mr. Fenster reminded Bert. "Now, you kids had better run along. And be sure you stay out of my way, while *I* solve this mystery!"

The crime reporter got up. He walked past

Bert and Flossie, totally ignoring them as he left the cubicle.

"I don't like him," said Flossie.

"Me neither," agreed Bert.

"This detective work is making me thirsty," Flossie said. "We passed a soda machine on the way here. Can I get a can?"

"Why not?" Bert said with a shrug. He was still fuming about what Amos Fenster had said.

As he and Flossie walked toward the soda machine, Bert promised himself that the Bobbseys would find the thief before that creep Amos Fenster did. They just had to!

When they reached the refreshment area, Bert dug in his jeans pocket for some coins. Though he was standing right in front of the soda machine, a blond girl about two years older than him edged him out of the way. "I'm in a hurry," she said as she pulled some change out of her purse.

Bert was annoyed with the girl, but Flossie didn't care. She thought the girl at the soda machine was beautiful. She particularly liked the girl's embroidered blouse, baggy pants, and bright, lime-colored sneakers.

"That's a great outfit," Flossie said. "Those sneakers are soooo wild!"

The blond girl ignored the compliment and punched a button on the soda machine. Her soda can made a *ka-chunk* sound as it rolled out to her waiting hand.

"I guess you didn't hear me," Flossie told her. "I said—"

"That you like my sneakers," the pretty girl said, cutting her off. "Like I'm supposed to care?"

Flossie's face turned red but not from embarrassment. "Who do you think you are?" she said angrily.

"I'm Suzy Cooper," the girl answered, looking down her nose at Flossie. "My father owns this newspaper."

"And *I'm* supposed to care?" Flossie shot back.

Bert smiled. If this spoiled rich kid thought she could bulldoze Flossie, she was wrong.

Suzy Cooper opened the pop top to her soda can and took a swig, ignoring Flossie.

Bert could have told the blond girl she was making a big mistake. Nobody ever ignored Flossie.

But just as his younger sister was about to give Suzy Cooper a piece of her mind, Bert heard the pounding of footsteps echoing down the hallway. Somebody was in a real hurry. Bert turned to see who was coming in their direction. "Look!" he shouted, pointing up the corridor.

Flossie gasped. It was Freddie. And he had a look of pure terror on his face!

4

A Close Call

"Hey! Wait up!" Flossie yelled as Freddie went tearing by. Forgetting all about Suzy Cooper, she took off after her brother.

Freddie skidded around a corner, making a wide left turn with Flossie hot on his trail. Then he spotted an open room, dashed inside, and dived behind a big photocopier. A second later, Flossie jammed in next to him.

"Who's chasing us?" she asked breathlessly. "Is it the thief?"

"Nobody is chasing *us,*" Freddie replied. He wiped the sweat from his forehead with his sleeve. "It's *me* she's after."

"Nan is chasing you?"

"No, dummy, the fashion editor. That Crane lady. She's the one."

"Did you prove she stole the clue?" Flossie asked hopefully.

"Nah. Before Nan could even ask about that," he said, "Helen Crane took one look at me, jumped up, and started hugging me and stuff. It was disgusting!"

"Why did she do that?" asked Flossie.

"You won't believe this. She pulled a pair of stupid-looking pajamas out of a drawer and said, 'Hurry up and put these on, young man. You'll make a great model for our children's fashion section.' "

"You? A model?" Flossie was flabbergasted.

"That's what *I* said," Freddie told her. "I got out of there as fast as I could. That Crane lady was yelling for me to come back. She started chasing after me, and I just took off. There's no way I'm going to wear those stupid pajamas."

"What did they look like?" Flossie asked.

"They had little frogs on them," Freddie said with a sour expression.

Flossie nodded. "I'd have run away, too," she said.

* * *

"That brother of yours is faster than a speeding bullet," Helen Crane told Nan after Freddie's sudden departure.

Nan chuckled. "You really scared him with those froggy pajamas," she said. "He'd have died if any of his friends saw him modeling them in the newspaper."

"Well, I guess I'll have to call someone from the agency." The fashion editor sighed and sat down on the edge of her desk. "Anyway, what can I do for you, Nan?"

"I wanted to ask a question," Nan began uneasily. The woman seemed friendly, and Nan didn't want to upset her if it wasn't necessary.

"Ask away," Helen Crane said breezily. She picked up a phone book and absently looked through the pages.

Nan hesitated. "I'm not quite sure how to put this," she said.

The fashion editor glanced at Nan and shook her head. "If you're going to ask me if I need a female model for teen clothes, I'm afraid the answer is no."

"Well, uh, that's not it," Nan stammered.

Helen Crane gave her a sidelong glance.

She doesn't believe me, Nan thought. I'm just going to have to ask her straight out. She took a deep breath and then blurted, "What were you doing all alone in my mom's office earlier this morning?"

The fashion editor slammed the phone book shut. "What are you suggesting?" she demanded coldly.

Nan refused to be bullied by Helen Crane's narrowed eyes and harsh tone. A good investigator, she told herself, doesn't let a suspect ask the questions.

"The last clue for the buried diamond contest was stolen out of my mom's office this morning," Nan said. She watched the fashion editor's face closely. "It was in a sealed envelope that Mr. Cooper gave her. Later, after you had been in my mom's office, the envelope was missing."

Helen Crane seemed to be genuinely amazed. "It was stolen? And—and you think *I* took it?" she sputtered. "Of all the idiotic ideas!"

"I didn't say that," corrected Nan. "I simply asked you what you were doing in my mom's office."

Helen Crane stood up, straightened her skirt, and cleared her throat. Finally, she said, "If you must know, I sneaked into your mother's office on purpose."

Nan's heart began to race. A confession!

"I waited until your mother was gone," continued the fashion editor. "Then I went inside and left a small birthday present for her on top of her computer screen. Your mother must have been very busy, because she didn't even notice it." She sniffed. "The box was wrapped in gold paper. Now are you satisfied?"

Nan swallowed. The fashion editor probably wouldn't lie about something that could be checked so easily. Still, Nan didn't remember seeing any gold packages in her mother's office.

Just then, Helen Crane looked at her watch. "I can't believe it!" she exclaimed. "It's already past twelve o'clock! I've got to get a young boy for that pajama shot. Couldn't you talk your little brother into modeling for me? Please?"

"Are you kidding?" said Nan. "Freddie is probably in hiding." Besides, she told herself, I have to find out if Helen Crane's story is true.

"It doesn't look like we were followed," Flossie whispered, peeking out from behind the copy machine.

Freddie shuddered at the memory of those frog-covered pajamas. "I'm not leaving."

SODA

"Well, I'm thirsty, and Bert was buying me a soda," Flossie said. "I'm going back."

"A soda?" Freddie asked, licking his dry lips. "What flavor?"

"Orange."

"Could I have some?"

Flossie pretended to think long and hard. "Okay," she said finally, "but just a sip."

They crawled out from behind the copier. Bert was leaning against the wall nearby. "I was wondering when you two were going to come out," he said.

"How come you didn't come after us faster?" asked Freddie. "Weren't you scared?"

"Scared of what? No one was chasing you," said Bert, taking a swallow from the can of orange soda in his hand.

"Hey, that's mine," Flossie protested.

"Sorry," Bert said with a laugh. "Come on, I'll buy you another one."

The three of them started back down the hall toward the brightly lit soda machine.

Freddie rushed ahead. Once he'd found a quarter in the coin return of a snack machine. He'd gotten into the habit of sticking his fingers in coin returns ever since, hoping to find more money.

This time, when he reached the machine, he spotted something on the floor. It was a crumpled envelope.

Freddie was stunned. Had he found the missing envelope with the diamond contest clue?

5

A Piece of the Puzzle

Freddie was already imagining the cheers and slaps on the back he would get for finding the missing diamond contest clue. His mother's birthday—and maybe even her job—would be saved. He'd be a hero!

Freddie picked up the crumpled envelope. As he tried to smooth it, he scratched his finger on a staple in the paper. "Ouch!" he cried. He stuck his finger in his mouth to ease the pain. A moment later, a sinking feeling came over him. The envelope had already been opened!

At first Freddie didn't see a thing when he looked inside the envelope.

Or did he?

Freddie blinked. Something had caught his eye. He looked again. There *was* something inside the envelope. The missing diamond clue was caught on the staple!

Freddie was so excited that he almost tore the envelope in half. He tugged the flap wider, working a torn scrap of paper free. The typed words on it read: "Guard your life under a—" That was all it said.

Freddie scratched his head. He had no idea what those five words meant. He didn't even know for sure if he had really found part of the clue. But if he had, then whoever had the other piece was missing an important part of the message. Well, Freddie thought smugly, at least now the clue won't be worth anything to the thief.

But Freddie also realized that *his* piece of the clue wasn't worth anything, either. Still, it was the first break in the mystery.

By this time, Bert and Flossie had caught up to Freddie. It had taken them longer to get to the machine because Flossie kept taking sips from Bert's half-empty soda can. Bert noticed Freddie staring at the crumpled piece of paper.

"Hey, what have you got there?" asked Bert.

Freddie couldn't wait to show Bert and

Flossie his important new discovery. But just then he saw Nan coming down the hall.

Uh-oh, he thought in a panic. What if she's got that Crane lady with her? Freddie quickly stuffed the envelope and the little scrap of paper into his back pocket and turned to run.

He had taken only about three steps before Bert snagged him by the arm. "Hey, Nan's coming. Where are you going?"

"Out of here," Freddie replied, trying to break his older brother's grip.

"But Nan might have some news," said Bert. "And we have to figure out our next move."

Freddie was doomed. He couldn't look. That Crane lady would dress him up in those stupid frog pajamas and take his picture. He would never hear the end of it from everybody at school. He'd have to pretend to be sick and stay home for at least a month. Maybe two.

"So, there you are," Nan said, giving Freddie a playful tap on the shoulder.

He had no choice. He turned to face his older sister, expecting to see Helen Crane standing next to her. But the fashion editor was nowhere in sight. He was safe! A big smile broke across his face.

"Here's the orange soda," Bert said, giving Freddie the soft drink. "Leave some for Nan."

With a sigh of relief, Freddie took a few big swallows.

"Well," Bert asked his twin, "is Helen Crane still a suspect?"

"I don't know," Nan said with a shrug. "She said she went into Mom's office to drop off a birthday present. And she did. I checked and found the gift just where she said she had left it. It got covered by a file folder."

"I wish she were guilty," Freddie said.

"What about Mr. Fenster?" Nan asked.

"I can't tell," Bert replied. "Not only did he say he was innocent, but he's trying to solve the case himself. He actually thinks *Mom* stole the clue!"

Nan was so surprised that her mouth dropped open. "Is he crazy or just plain stupid?" she asked.

"Both," Flossie said with feeling.

"Mr. Fenster isn't our biggest problem, though," Bert said. He glanced at his watch. "We have only four hours and twenty-six minutes left to find the clue!"

Nan felt defeated. They couldn't come up with any more leads or suspects. Right now, they could have four years and twenty-six days to find the thief and the missing clue for all the good it would do them. They were stuck.

But Nan wasn't going to give up.

"We've got to think," she said finally. "We promised Mom we'd solve this mystery for her birthday. We can't let her down."

"Maybe we should try to glue the glass dog back together," Freddie suggested. "It might not be as badly smashed as we think."

The other Bobbseys stared at him.

"Uh . . . just kidding," Freddie said quickly.

"Rex Sleuther never gives up on a case," Bert said. "And neither do we."

Then Freddie suddenly remembered the envelope in his back pocket. "Hey!" he said.

That was as far as he got. A big, burly man, with a scar slicing down his left cheek, barged past them to get to the soda machine. He looked mean, and the Bobbseys quickly scattered out of his way.

The man didn't seem to notice them. He put his leather briefcase down on the floor and unzipped it. Then he slipped the magazine he was carrying inside. With his hands now free, he dug in his pockets, muttering about never having change when he needed it.

Trying not to stare, Nan looked away from the man. Her gaze drifted to the magazine that was still sticking out of the man's open briefcase. A twinkle of light caught her eye.

SODA

That's strange, she thought. Why should something be twinkling inside a dark briefcase?

Nan edged closer to get a better look. When she saw what was in the bag, her eyes bulged. There, right next to the magazine, was a plastic bag full of tiny glittering nuggets. Could they be the diamonds? she wondered.

Nan nudged Bert and nodded toward the briefcase. He followed her gaze and shook his head slightly. Then he looked again. He had no idea who this tough-looking man was, but he was now their number-one suspect!

6

A Dangerous Place

Just a few moments earlier, the Bobbseys had been stumped by this case. Now it looked as if they were standing right next to the thief! He had worked fast. First, he had stolen the clue and figured out where the diamonds were hidden. And now he had come back to the scene of the crime, pretending nothing had happened!

The man had already gotten his soda. He opened the can, picked up his briefcase, and walked away.

Nan looked at Bert. "What should we do?" she asked in a low voice. "We have no way of stopping him."

The man was huge. He was very tall, and he looked as if he weighed almost as much as the soda machine.

"Come on," Bert whispered. "Let's go after him."

Nan signaled for Flossie and Freddie to follow along.

"Where are we going?" Flossie said loudly.

Nan leaned down and told Flossie and Freddie what was in the big man's briefcase.

"THE DIAMONDS!" Freddie exclaimed.

The instant he said it, Freddie slapped his hand over his mouth. The Bobbseys all turned their eyes toward the man with the briefcase. He didn't act as if he'd heard Freddie. He simply kept on walking.

He's probably thinking about how he's going to spend the money he gets from selling those stolen jewels, Bert thought. *Well, you can just forget about it, mister,* he vowed silently. *We're not going to let you get away with it!*

The twins stayed ten yards behind the man as he led them past the art department. That's when Freddie saw a hand reach out for Flossie from an open doorway.

"Hey!" he shouted to Flossie. "Watch out!"

Everyone turned to look, including the big man whom they were following.

Just then, Mrs. Bobbsey emerged from the art department, putting her arm around Flossie. "It's only me," said their mother. "What's all the fuss about?"

"Uh, nothing," said Freddie, blushing.

"Any luck yet?" Mrs. Bobbsey asked Nan and Bert hopefully.

Bert turned to look back up the hallway. The man was gone!

"Not yet," he said quickly. "We think we've got a pretty good suspect, but we have to find him again! Come on, guys!"

With Bert in the lead, the Bobbsey twins ran down the corridor until it crossed another hallway. Nan looked left. Bert looked right.

Nan thought she caught sight of the man turning down another hallway. "This way!" she called out.

They passed the photo lab and the computer room. Then they hurried past the cafeteria. "I'm hungry," Flossie announced. Before the others could stop her, she skidded to a stop, turned, and marched right into the busy lunchroom. Bert chased after her.

"I've been wondering where you kids have been," said Amos Fenster, the crime reporter. He was sitting at a table with an open notebook in front of him. "I've been studying my notes on this case," he said smugly, "and your mother had better watch out. She's still the leading suspect."

"Oh, yeah?" Flossie said angrily. "Well, what about the big guy—"

"Flossie!" Bert warned from behind her.

"Oops," said Flossie. She realized how close she had come to making a big mistake.

Bert took a deep breath. He had stopped his sister just in time. There was no way he was going to let the crime reporter beat them to the thief.

"Do you guys know something?" Mr. Fenster asked, frowning.

"Us?" Bert answered innocently. "Hey, we're just kids, right? What could we know?" He grabbed Flossie's hand and they quickly left the cafeteria.

"Come on," Bert said once they were out in the hallway. "We've got to catch up to Nan and Freddie. They went that way," he added, pointing down a narrow corridor.

After a long run that took them past the newspaper's loading dock, Bert led Flossie toward a set of big, swinging doors. Nan and Freddie were waiting for them.

"Did you lose him?" Bert asked.

"Nope. He's in there," Nan said, nodding toward the swinging doors.

All of a sudden, a loud hum of machinery made the floor vibrate under their feet.

"Boy, it's really noisy here," Flossie said.

Nan slowly opened one of the doors just a few inches wide to see what had caused the racket.

"What's in there?" asked Flossie, unable to push past Bert and Freddie.

"The printing presses," Nan replied. She was awed by the giant machines in the huge room.

"We've got to keep the thief in sight," said Bert. "Come on, let's go in."

They entered the big room. Bert felt totally out of place. He knew that they would probably get stopped by one of the workers soon. But they had to find that thief—and fast!

"Wow, this is something," said Freddie. He stared at the giant rolling presses. They were as big as trucks. Then he spotted enormous spools of paper that were four times his size. He wanted to climb them. "This is a great place," he told Flossie.

Flossie didn't look so sure.

Nan spotted their suspect at the controls of a

rolling press. "He's over there," she told the others, pointing. The Bobbseys set off toward the large man, but they didn't get very far.

"What are you kids doing here?" demanded a voice from behind them. It was a man with ink on his hands.

"Uh . . . well . . ." Bert began awkwardly.

"We're on a field trip," Flossie piped up.

"Really?" the man asked with a smile. "That's great! Everybody should learn how a newspaper is really born. Others may write what's in it, but it's the printers—folks like me—who put it on paper."

"Is that man over there a printer, too?" asked Nan. She nodded toward the man they had followed.

"Bascomb? Sure."

"Could you show us what he's doing with that machine?" Bert asked.

"My pleasure," the man replied. He led them right to their suspect.

"These kids are taking a tour of the printing presses," the man told him.

Mr. Bascomb looked up and scowled. "They shouldn't be in here, Danny. This is a *dangerous* place," he added darkly.

Flossie shivered.

LAKEPORT
NEWS

Meanwhile, Bert edged closer to Mr. Bascomb's briefcase, which was on the floor. It was still open. Bert could plainly see the bag full of glittering gems.

"You worry too much, Bascomb," Danny said. "You're always afraid you'll lose your job. Those payments on your new boat must be running you dry."

Aha! thought Bert. There's the motive. This Bascomb guy needs money badly. Now all they'd have to do was prove he was the thief. Bert began inching closer to the briefcase.

An angry look crossed Mr. Bascomb's face. "Worry about your own job, Danny," he said. "Showing nosy kids around isn't what you get paid for."

Danny shoved his hands in his pockets. "All right, you kids," he said. "I guess you'd better leave. I ought to get back to my job."

By this time, Bert was right next to the briefcase. He knew he had to do something in a hurry or lose his chance to catch the crook. It was now or never.

Bert thought fast. Before Mr. Bascomb could react, he pretended to lose his balance. Then he "accidentally" kicked the briefcase over. Just as he had hoped, the sparkling little gems went flying from the briefcase. They spilled all over the floor.

"The diamonds!" Freddie and Flossie shouted in unison. They dived to the floor and tried to scoop up the gleaming gems.

Then Danny gasped in surprise. Mr. Bascomb had suddenly lunged right toward Freddie and Flossie!

7

Crystal Clear

"Look out!" Nan shouted.

Thanks to their sister's warning, Freddie and Flossie saw Mr. Bascomb dive at them. They rolled out of the way, and the huge man landed with a *whomp* on the floor.

The hard fall didn't stop Mr. Bascomb at all. "Give me those!" he demanded of Freddie and Flossie. They were still shoving the shiny stones into their pockets.

"We would, if they were yours," Flossie said.

"What do you mean, if they're mine?" Mr.

Bascomb said angrily. He grabbed Flossie by the arm.

"Stop that, Bascomb," said Danny. He pulled the big man's hand off Flossie. "Don't lose your temper. She's just a kid."

"I don't care who or what she is. These four brats are stealing my crystals."

Bert froze, dropping one of the shiny gems. "Crystals?" he asked.

"Yeah," Mr. Bascomb said. "I bought them for the bottom of my aquarium."

By this time a dozen workers had come running over.

Meanwhile, Nan examined one of the clear, shiny stones. Maybe Mr. Bascomb is lying, she thought. I've got to find out for sure.

"Just a minute," Nan said loudly, getting everyone's attention. "I read in school that diamonds are the strongest stones on earth. So, I'm going to rub one of them on the floor and see what happens."

"Don't do it," the big man begged.

"Afraid we've got you, huh?" Nan said. She scraped the stone against the floor. The glittering gem quickly split into three pieces. It really was a crystal.

"You broke it," said Mr. Bascomb with a sigh. "I asked you not to do that."

Nan flushed deeply. "Did we ever make a mistake!" she said.

She gave the pieces of broken crystal to Mr. Bascomb. Freddie and Flossie emptied their pockets and gave him the stones they had collected.

Bert shook his head. "We're really sorry, Mr. Bascomb," he said. "We thought you stole the last clue in the diamond contest. We were hoping these crystals were the five thousand dollars in diamonds."

The big man could hardly believe his ears. "Me? A thief? Is this a joke?" he said. Then, he surprised the twins by suddenly giving a hearty laugh. "Man, if only those crystals really *were* diamonds," he said. "Now that would have been something!"

The assembled crowd agreed.

"Diamonds that size would be worth over a million dollars!"a woman in the group called out.

"I'd quit my job in a flash!" Mr. Bascomb smiled broadly.

The crowd roared with laughter.

Bert and Nan looked at each other. They felt like fools.

Mr. Bascomb became very friendly. He took Flossie by the hand. "I hope I didn't hurt your arm," he said.

"Oh, no," she told him. "I'm too tough for you to hurt me."

Mr. Bascomb chuckled. "You're a good kid," he said. "I like you."

"I like you, too," Flossie said.

Nan noticed that the crowd was beginning to break up. She also spotted a big clock on the wall. "Oh, no," she said with a gasp. "It's almost ten after one!"

Bert heard Nan and frowned. "We have less than four hours left."

"Something's going on over by the door," Freddie interrupted.

The Bobbseys heard a loud voice, but they couldn't make out the words. Someone was telling the workers to get back to their jobs.

"It's a girl," said Freddie.

"You're always goofing off," the girl shouted. "My father is going to hear about this."

No one moved any faster.

"Don't think I won't tell him," she insisted. The girl stamped one of her feet on the floor.

The workers continued to ignore her as they went back to their stations.

Flossie saw the girl walking their way. She narrowed her eyes and said, "It's that stuck-up Suzy Cooper!"

The publisher's daughter stopped right in front of the Bobbseys. She put her hands on her hips. "Who gave you permission to wander around this newspaper?" she demanded.

"Our mother works here," Nan explained. "She's Mary Bobbsey."

"*She* works here, not *you*. And *I* work here, not *you*."

Flossie stuck out her chin. "What do you do that's so great?" she asked.

"I do lots of things," Suzy Cooper said. "Every Saturday I run errands for my dad. And my most important job is watching what comes in over the wire."

"What's 'the wire'?" Flossie asked. She was immediately sorry she had opened her mouth. The publisher's daughter grinned because she knew something Flossie didn't.

"It's news from all over the country that's sent here electronically," Suzy Cooper said. "It gets printed on computer paper. I check the machines and take the wire service news to the managing editor. Then I go home at two-thirty. That's *my* job. But *you* have no business here."

"Yes, we do," Freddie said simply.

The publisher's daughter turned to glare at him.

"We're on an important case," he explained. "Somebody stole the last clue for the diamond contest from our mom's office, and—"

Suddenly, Freddie remembered the torn paper he had found by the soda machine. He had forgotten it in the excitement of following Mr. Bascomb. Freddie quickly pulled it from his back pocket. "—and all we have to do now is find out who has the other piece of this clue."

Nan spun Freddie around. "Where did you find that?" she asked excitedly.

"It was stapled to an envelope that had Mom's name on it," Freddie said. "I found it all crumpled up by the soda machine."

Nan, Bert, and Flossie crowded around Freddie. Suzy Cooper was just as curious as the Bobbseys. "Let me see that," she insisted, trying to push past Nan.

Unable to get a good look, the publisher's daughter stepped back. "You guys couldn't solve a jigsaw puzzle, let alone an important theft," she said nastily.

"You don't know anything," Flossie shot back. "We'll solve this case. You'll see. We promised our mom that we would catch the thief. We're going to return the clue for her birthday. We won't let her down."

"You shouldn't make promises you can't keep," said the blond girl with a sneer.

Freddie didn't like the way Suzy Cooper was talking to his twin. "We already have part of the clue," Freddie said, waving the scrap of paper. He shoved it into his back pocket.

The publisher's daughter looked at the clock on the wall and grinned. "You had better hurry up if you're going to solve your mystery," she said. "In just three hours and thirty-two minutes, tomorrow's paper goes to press." Then she turned and marched away.

"Is she a spoiled brat, or what?" Bert shook his head.

"She sure is," Nan replied with a sigh.

"Well, we've finally found someone worse than Flossie," kidded Freddie. His twin gave him a playful poke in the ribs.

"There's one thing Suzy Cooper was right about," Bert said seriously.

"I know," agreed Nan. "We're running out of time. We can't just hang around and gossip about the publisher's daughter all day."

"You just said something that gives me an idea," said Bert thoughtfully.

"I did?" asked Nan. "What?"

"You said 'gossip.'"

"So?" Nan frowned.

"Well, we're already pretty sure that the theft was an inside job," Bert began slowly. "What we need now is a motive for the person who stole the clue. Maybe the newspaper's gossip columnist could give us a lead. It's worth a try."

"It sure is," said Nan. "But who is the gossip columnist?"

"I know," Flossie said brightly. "It's Bill Billius. Susie Larker's mom reads his column every day. He knows *everything* that's happening in town. So he just has to know about the people who work right here at the *Lakeport News.*"

"I can't believe it," said Freddie. "She's making sense."

Flossie gave Freddie another poke in the ribs.

"I'm not a punching bag," Freddie complained. Just the same, he was smiling.

They hurried out of the huge room full of printing presses and retraced their steps past the loading dock, the cafeteria, and the computer room.

When they saw a clerk, Nan asked, "Where can we find Bill Billius's office?"

"Walk straight to the last corridor at the far side of the building. Then make a left," the clerk said. "You'll find Bill about halfway down that final corridor."

Once or twice, Bert thought they were being followed. There were a lot of filing cabinets along the busy hallway. They made good places to hide. Then Bert was sure he saw Amos Fenster, the crime reporter, ducking behind one of those cabinets. Another time, he saw only a shadow as someone slinked out of view behind a group of secretaries. Or maybe his imagination was playing tricks on him.

The Bobbseys reached the last corridor and turned left. Just then, the lights went off. The twins were plunged into total blackness!

8

Blackout!

It was so dark that Bert lost all sense of direction. He walked right into the wall, face first. "Ouch!" he said, rubbing his nose. Freddie had wisely stopped in his tracks. But someone bumped into him, knocking him to the right. At first, he thought it was Flossie who had pushed him. Then he lost his balance and fell into his twin. They both tumbled over.

"Is that you, Freddie?" Flossie demanded. The two of them were tangled in each other's arms and legs.

"Yes," Freddie said. "And stop kicking me!"

"That's the second time today you've knocked me down," Flossie said disgustedly.

"It wasn't my fault," Freddie answered. "Somebody pushed me."

"I think I've found the box with the circuit breaker!" a nearby voice cried out.

Suddenly, the lights flashed back on.

The woman who had found the circuit breaker walked past the Bobbseys. Her fellow workers in the hallway cheered.

"I don't understand it," Bert said. "But I think someone was following us right before the lights blacked out. We'd better be careful."

Nan glanced quickly around. "I wonder who it was," she said.

"I bet it was that crime reporter, Mr. Fenster," said Bert. "I just wish I knew for sure." He looked at his watch. "That's more time lost," he said. "We'd better get a move on. It's almost a quarter to two. The time is flying!"

With Bert in the lead, the Bobbseys raced down the corridor to Bill Billius's office. Luckily, the gossip columnist was there. He was sitting at his computer, writing.

Mr. Billius was a tall, rumpled-looking, bearded man. The twins told him all about the case. "You'd be surprised how many people

might steal to get their hands on five thousand dollars' worth of diamonds," he said. "I could name a few for you."

"We wish you would," said Nan. "We sure could use a lead."

"First," Mr. Billius said, "please understand that I'm not accusing anybody of stealing that clue off your mother's desk. I'm just passing along some of my observations about my fellow *Lakeport News* employees. Understand?"

"We understand," said Nan, nodding.

"Fine." Mr. Billius scratched his head. "Helen Crane, the fashion editor, is crazy for jewelry," he began. "Especially diamonds. When she's all dressed up, she practically drips with them. But nobody knows if they're real or fake."

"She was seen coming out of our mom's office this morning," Nan explained. "But she was only dropping off a present. And I saw the box. She wasn't lying."

Bert frowned. "Maybe when she left the gift," he said, "she saw the clue on Mom's desk and decided to take it. It might not have been a planned theft."

"Hmmm," said Nan.

"Of course," the gossip columnist continued, "there are others you might consider.

For instance, there's the new reporter who covers the crime beat—"

"Amos Fenster," interrupted Bert.

"That's correct," Mr. Billius said. He sounded surprised. "My, you Bobbseys seem to know all the right people. Anyway, he's pretty nosy. Someone who worked with him at another newspaper said Fenster would do anything for a good story."

"Or maybe even create a crime that he could solve himself?" asked Bert.

"I really don't know," said Mr. Billius.

"Maybe the *Lakeport News* has a ghost," Freddie said, his eyes growing wide. "You know, a spooky creature that everybody knows about but nobody has ever seen."

"I don't think so," said Mr. Billius. He looked amused. "We don't have a ghost," he continued, "but some people think the publisher's daughter, Suzy, is a pest."

"I don't blame them," said Flossie.

Mr. Billius nodded. "On Saturdays, holidays, whenever she's off from school, that girl is around. She annoys almost everyone at the paper."

"That's no surprise," Flossie said.

"You really don't like her, do you, Flossie?" Nan said. "What did she do to you?"

"I was real nice to her at the soda machine," Flossie said. "But she was mean to me for no reason at all."

Freddie frowned. "At the soda machine?" he asked.

Flossie nodded. "That's where I first saw her."

"That's where I found that torn piece of the clue," Freddie said slowly. He reached into his back pocket. It was empty!

"The paper's gone!" Freddie cried.

"Maybe you lost it when you fell during the blackout," said Flossie.

"I didn't fall," Freddie corrected her. "I was *pushed!*"

"Which means," said Nan, "that maybe the blackout wasn't an accident. Maybe the lights were turned off on purpose."

"Why?" asked Flossie.

"So the thief could jump on Freddie and steal the other half of the clue," Bert said.

"If that's true," said Mr. Billius, "then the thief now has everything he needs to find the diamonds."

"But now we have everything *we* need to find the thief!" Nan said triumphantly.

9

On the Trail of the Thief

"What time is it, Bert?" asked Nan.

"It's eight minutes after two," Bert said.

"Oh, no! There's barely enough time!" Nan cried. "We've got to rush!" She thanked Mr. Billius for his help and hurried out the door.

Bert, Freddie, and Flossie followed closely behind her.

"I'm really glad we solved this case," said Freddie as they rushed down the hall.

"Me, too," agreed Flossie.

"Yeah. I was getting worried there for a while," admitted Bert. "But one thing still bothers me," he added. "Who did it?"

"I'll tell you in a second," Nan called over her shoulder. She ran down the corridor past several startled newspaper employees. After a sharp right turn, she stopped short in front of an empty office.

"Quick. Everybody in here," she said. She pointed to the empty room. Then she turned out the light, leaving the four of them hidden in the dark with the door open just a crack.

Nan peered out into the hallway. "Besides us, only one person knew that Freddie had found the torn piece of the clue," she whispered. "Suzy Cooper."

"That's right!" said Bert. "She was there when Freddie showed us the clue."

"She must have seen him put it back in his pocket," continued Nan. "And remember, Bert, that you thought we were being followed?"

He nodded.

"Just a short time later there was the blackout," said Nan.

"That's when somebody knocked Freddie over," Bert chimed in.

"See, I told you it wasn't my fault," Freddie said to Flossie.

"Suzy Cooper probably didn't mean to knock you down," said Nan. "But she definitely wanted to pick your pocket and take your half of the clue."

"Are you sure?" Flossie asked. Her head was spinning from all these details.

"No, I'm not," said Nan. "We've been wrong before. After all, we were positive that Mr. Bascomb had stolen the diamonds. We could be wrong again."

"But how is hiding in here going to prove that Suzy Cooper stole the clue?" asked Freddie.

"Because the wire service room is across the hall," Nan said. "And—"

"—Suzy Cooper takes the wire service news to the managing editor by two-thirty," Bert finished. "It's her last job of the day."

"How does that prove that she's the thief?" asked Freddie, confused.

Nan smiled. "It doesn't," she said. "But if I'm right about her, she'll leave the building in a few minutes and lead us to the diamonds."

"Sshhh," Bert warned. "I think she's coming."

The publisher's daughter hurried into the wire service room as four pairs of eyes watched her every move.

Suzy Cooper tore a long sheet of paper from each of the machines that had printed out the day's important events. She made a sloppy pile of the papers, folding them under her arm. Then she practically flew down the hall toward the managing editor's office.

"Come on," said Nan. "We've got to follow her. But if she knows we're on her tail, she won't lead us to the diamonds. So make sure you stay out of sight."

Suzy Cooper sneaked out of the *Lakeport News* building through a side exit. She glanced around.

"Which way is she going?" Flossie asked from behind a row of hedges.

"Down Pine Street," Bert replied.

"Let's go after her," Freddie said, jumping up.

Bert pulled him back down. "Not so fast, kiddo," he said. "Let her get a block ahead of us first."

The publisher's daughter walked quickly. At the end of Pine Street, she turned onto Spruce.

"Now!" said Bert.

The Bobbseys ran down the block until they neared the corner. Then they slid behind a parked car and searched Spruce Street.

"I see her," said Nan. "She's on the other side of the street. Over there, by that sprinkler."

"We can't let her get too far ahead," said Bert. "Come on, let's go."

The Bobbseys stayed within a block of Suzy Cooper as she turned onto Sycamore Drive. They hid behind anything they could find: fences, bushes, even garbage cans.

"Where do you think she's going?" asked Freddie as they reached the parking lot of the Starlight Diner.

"I can't tell yet," said Bert. "She could be going almost anywhere."

Suzy Cooper passed a grocery store, a post office, and a pet shop. Then they heard the sound of church bells. They rang three times.

"It's three o'clock already," said Flossie. "Only two hours left!"

Finally Suzy Cooper turned onto a street full of big houses. But when she reached the third house on the left, she went inside.

Nan frowned. "This can't be right," she said. "The diamonds can't be inside somebody's house."

"Wait here," said Bert. He ran up the block and looked at the mailbox in front of the house. Then he ran back and slid down next to Nan. "It's *her* house!" he said. "It says 'Cooper' on the mailbox!"

"She just went home?" Flossie asked,

puzzled. "Does this mean she's not the thief?"

Nan didn't know what to say.

Bert looked at his watch. It was just past three-fifteen.

"Should we go back and tell Mom that we flopped?" asked Freddie.

Before either Bert or Nan could answer, Suzy Cooper walked out the front door of her house.

"Get down," Bert said to the others.

"Why are we doing this if she's not the thief?" asked Freddie.

"Because she's carrying a small pail and shovel," said Bert excitedly. "She's going to dig something up. And my guess is it's the diamonds!"

They followed Suzy Cooper for another twenty minutes. They passed the Lakeport movie theater, two video stores, and blocks and blocks of houses.

Suddenly, Nan realized where the publisher's daughter was heading. "She's going to the beach!" Nan announced.

"Why?" said Freddie. "It's too cold to go swimming. He looked up at the gray autumn sky.

"Maybe she's going fishing," suggested Flossie.

"She's fishing, all right. Fishing for diamonds," said Nan. "Remember that part of the clue Freddie found? It said 'Guard your life.' The only place you can find a lifeguard is at the beach. And the lake is just a block from here."

A few minutes later, the Bobbseys were hiding behind a sand dune.

"She went right for the lifeguard stand," said Bert.

"What's she reading?" asked Freddie, peeking over the dune.

"It must be the clue," guessed Nan. "She taped the two pieces together."

"She's digging in the sand," reported Flossie.

Then Bert noticed that Suzy Cooper had dropped her shovel. "I think she found something," he said.

"Come on! Let's get her!" shouted Nan.

They climbed over the sand dune and charged like a troop of cavalry. Before Suzy Cooper knew it, she was surrounded by Bobbseys. In her hands, in a shallow pit in the sand, was a small wooden treasure chest.

"Wh-what are you doing here?" the publisher's daughter stammered.

"Solving a mystery," said Flossie with a grin.

Suzy Cooper looked frightened. She had been caught red-handed.

"Are you going to turn me in to the police?" she asked in a shaky voice. "I mean, I didn't actually steal the diamonds," she added. "After all, they still belong to my father."

"I wonder if your dad would see it that way," Nan said softly.

The older girl said nothing. She blushed and tears formed in her eyes. For the first time, Suzy Cooper seemed like a real person.

Nan began to feel almost sorry for the spoiled girl. "I don't know what to do," Nan told the others. "Maybe we should take her back to the paper to see Mom."

"Not before we see what's in that box," insisted Flossie.

"Good idea," agreed Nan. Suzy Cooper silently handed her the little wooden treasure chest.

Nan opened it quickly. Inside the box was a beautiful, sparkling necklace on a black velvet cushion. The rest of the Bobbseys crowded around to see. Suzy Cooper tried to back away, but Bert clamped his hand around her wrist. She didn't move.

The necklace was dazzling, even in the dim afternoon light.

"Let me wear it!" Flossie cried.

Nan smiled and hung it around her little sister's neck. Flossie ran to the edge of the lake and gazed at her reflection in the water. "I look like a princess!" she declared.

"Yeah, and I'm a wrestling champ," Freddie muttered under his breath.

"Flossie," Nan said gently, "the diamonds aren't real, remember? There's a note in the box." Nan read it aloud: " 'Come to the *Lakeport News* with this glass look-alike of the winning prize. Claim your genuine five-thousand-dollar diamond necklace in a special ceremony.' "

"Oh, rats," said Flossie.

They put the fake diamond necklace back in the treasure chest and buried it again.

Then Nan turned to Suzy Cooper. "Can we have the clue now?"

Defeated, the publisher's daughter handed the taped piece of paper over to Nan.

"Thanks," said Nan.

"Don't thank me yet," Suzy Cooper replied. "You've got to get that clue back before the paper goes to press."

Bert looked at his watch. "It's ten minutes after four!" he said in alarm.

10

Deadline!

"All we have to do is call Mom at the newspaper. We can read her the clue over the phone," Nan said.

"We passed a gas station a few blocks back," Bert said excitedly. "There was a telephone booth there."

They found the gas station five minutes later. "I've got some change," Nan said. She put the money into the phone and held the receiver to her ear. There was no dial tone. "It's broken!" Nan announced.

"There was a phone at the movie theater," said Flossie.

But when they got to the theater, a man was already using the phone. They had to wait.

And wait.

Finally, Bert spoke up. "We need to make a call," he said. "Are you almost finished?"

The man scowled at Bert. He had a toothpick in his mouth. "I'll be finished when I hang up, and not before."

"Let's look for another telephone," said Nan.

But the video store next door didn't have one. They finally found another phone booth, but that was broken, too.

"The paper goes to press in thirty-two minutes. We'll never make it!" Bert wailed.

"I wish we had our bikes," Freddie said.

"Or a flying carpet," said Flossie.

"Would a shortcut do?" Suzy Cooper asked softly.

"You know a faster way back to the paper?" Bert asked.

Suzy nodded. "We could cut through the golf course behind the grocery store," she said. "I know the way. Do you want me to show it to you?"

Bert didn't answer right away. Neither did the others.

"Oh," Suzy said, sounding embarrassed. "I get it. You don't trust me."

"You *did* try to ruin the contest," said Nan. "And if we don't get back in time with the clue, the contest will still be ruined."

"But you caught me," said the publisher's daughter. "And if I help you save the contest, maybe my dad won't be so angry with me when he finds out. Besides," she added, "I'm glad you're not going to turn me over to the police." She looked at Bert, and then Nan, straight in the eye. "Please," she said, "let me help."

Nan stepped away and signaled to the others. Once she was sure they were outside of Suzy Cooper's hearing, Nan whispered, "She could be lying."

"What choice do we have?" asked Bert. "She's our only hope of getting to the newspaper on time."

"Let's vote," said Nan. "Who's in favor of taking the shortcut?"

They all raised their hands. Even Flossie.

Suzy Cooper led the way as they raced across the community golf course. They circled around a pond. Then they followed a path through the woods next to the golf course. They broke through the trees. Now they were only three blocks from the *Lakeport News,* so they hurried even faster.

"Eleven minutes left!" Bert called out breathlessly.

They dashed through the newspaper's parking lot. Then they streaked through the building, toward Mrs. Bobbsey's office.

Freddie and Flossie both cried out as they reached the door, "We've got it! We've got it!"

Nan took the clue out of her pocket. Then Freddie grabbed it out of his older sister's hands. At that very moment, Flossie also reached for the clue. Both of the younger twins pulled on the fragile, taped piece of paper.

"I want to give it to Mom!" shouted Freddie.

"No, me," insisted Flossie.

"One wrecked present per birthday is enough," said Bert. He plucked the clue from the hands of both younger twins.

He was about to give it to his mother, but then he stopped and handed it to Suzy Cooper. "Here," he said. "Maybe you ought to do this. We never would have made it back here in time without you."

Suzy smiled gratefully at Bert.

"Mrs. Bobbsey," Suzy began, "I stole this clue from your desk this morning. You walked out with my dad, and I just reached out and took it. It was a dumb thing to do. I'm really sorry."

The phone rang. Mrs. Bobbsey picked it up and listened for a moment. Then she smiled.

Mrs. Bobbsey covered the mouthpiece. "It's the managing editor," she said. "She was worried that the clue wouldn't make it into the paper. But she didn't know my kids were on the case." She took the clue from Suzy Cooper's hand. "Two minutes left?" she said into the phone. "Here, let me read it to you."

When their mom hung up, Flossie looked at the clock on the wall. It was one minute to five.

Finally, Mrs. Bobbsey turned to Suzy Cooper. "Your father is going to want to know why you did this," she said. "In fact, I'd like to know myself."

"Everyone at the paper ignores me," Suzy said sadly. "I mean, I'm just the boss's kid. But I figured nobody would ignore me if I messed up the contest."

"You're right," Mrs. Bobbsey said. "You wouldn't have been ignored. But you wouldn't have been liked, either."

"So what?" Suzy replied bitterly. "Today's my birthday. My dad was too busy to spend it with me." She looked at the floor. "I know it was stupid, but I thought he'd have to come back if the contest was ruined. But now nobody will ever like me," she said, holding back a sob.

"That's not true," Nan said. "I like you."

"So do I," said Bert.

"Me, too," added Freddie.

Everybody looked at Flossie. After a long pause, a big smile crossed her face. "I think you're neat," she said.

"Thanks," said Suzy. But then she frowned. "I really put you on the spot, Mrs. Bobbsey. You would have been in a lot of trouble if I hadn't been caught in time. Can you forgive me?"

The twins looked at their mother hopefully.

Mrs. Bobbsey didn't hesitate. "Of course you're forgiven, Suzy. And though you'll probably be punished, your father will forgive you, too. I'll explain everything to him."

Suddenly, there was a loud knock on the door.

"Come in," Mrs. Bobbsey called out.

Amos Fenster, the crime reporter, walked inside. "I have good news," he said smugly. "I have plenty of leads on this missing diamond clue. So far, Mrs. Bobbsey, you're in the clear." He turned to the twins. "As for you kids," he said, "you might as well give up. You haven't

got a chance of breaking this case. I'll have it nailed by Tuesday at the latest."

"Really?" said Bert. His eyes twinkled as he looked at Flossie.

"Are you surprised?" asked Mr. Fenster.

"Not as surprised as you're going to be," said Flossie. She winked at Bert.

Mr. Fenster frowned. "What do you mean?"

"We found the clue," said Bert. "It's running in tomorrow's newspaper. Just the way it's supposed to."

The crime reporter was stunned. "How did you find it?" he demanded.

"We had some help," said Nan, nodding toward the publisher's daughter. "We couldn't have done it without Suzy."

"I can't believe it," Mr. Fenster muttered. He left the office quickly.

"Well, we've got some celebrating to do," said Mrs. Bobbsey. "How about all of us—you, too, Suzy—going to dinner with Dad tonight?"

Everyone cheered and called out, "HAPPY BIRTHDAY!"

Mrs. Bobbsey hugged them all. "You kids really did save my birthday," she said.

"Hey, nothing to it," said Freddie. "We even had a whole minute left."